THE MYSTERY OF THE SECRET
HAIR OIL FORMULA

Asha Nehemiah is an author based in Bangalore. Her books for children include *Granny's Sari*, *The Rajah's Moustache*, *Zigzag and Other Stories*, and *Sir Lawley's Ghost and Other Stories*.

The Mystery of the Secret Hair Oil Formula

Asha Nehemiah

Illustrations Amit Vachharajani

SCHOLASTIC

New York Toronto London Auckland Sydney
New Delhi Hong Kong

For Vinod
who looks at life through fun-tinted spectacles
and is the funniest person I know

Text © 2006 Asha Nehemiah
Illustrations © 2006 Amit Vachharajani

Published by Scholastic India Pvt. Ltd.
A subsidiary of Scholastic Inc., New York, 10012 (USA).
Publishers since 1920, with international operations in Canada, Australia, New Zealand, the United Kingdom, Mexico, India, Argentina, and Hong Kong.

For information regarding permission, write to:
Scholastic India Pvt. Ltd.
Golf View Corporate Tower-A, 3rd Floor,
DLF Phase-V, Gurgaon-122002 (India)

Typeset by Mantra Virtual Services Pvt. Ltd.

First edition: September 2006
Reprint: February; May 2009; January 2010; May; July
November 2012; February 2014; January 2015; February 2016
September 2017

ISBN-13: 978-81-7655-565-4

Printed at Dot Scan Pvt. Ltd; New Delhi

Contents

Wondergro Supersonic Hair Tonic

Malu Paati was running out of places where she could hide the secret paper. The thieves had broken into her house several times already, but luckily, they had not found the secret paper so far. When she had hidden it in her kitchen, cleverly folded to fit between two slices of bread in the bread box, the burglars had searched her bedroom instead. Then, she had shifted the secret paper into her bedroom. She had removed the batteries from her torch and put the paper in the battery compartment. That was the time the burglars had raided her kitchen, emptying the sacks of rice and onions and even pouring out the coconut oil from the jar in their frantic search for the paper.

At the top of this most secret paper, Malu Paati's father, once the most famous research scientist in the valley of Mounashrampur, had

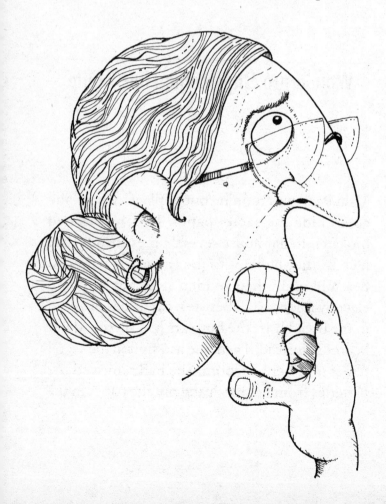

pencilled these words in a shaky handwriting quite unlike his usual bold scrawl: 'Don't let this paper out of your sight, Malu. Can't have it falling into the wrong hands'. Below that, he had faintly signed off, 'Appa'.

The paper contained a secret formula for making an amazing hair oil that could make hair grow even on bald heads. When she first got hold of the secret formula, Malu Paati had spent many months trying to make the herbal hair oil. It seemed an impossible task at first. One effort ended in a small explosion and purplish-blue pulp splattering all over the kitchen. Another trial produced a silvery-grey mixture which rumbled and swirled quite terrifyingly once it was put in a bottle—almost as if there was a thundercloud or a magic spirit held there! But after many attempts, Malu Paati had succeeded.

Then, she chose Veerapandi, the wrestling champion and the baldest man in town, to try out the first bottle. He applied the hair oil generously on his shiny bald head and now the champion wrestler had a ponytail that needed to be tied up in a topknot the size of a large coconut.

It was, indeed, a most wonderful and amazing hair oil. Bald people who used it soon needed weekly haircuts and short-haired people quickly

grew hair long enough to sit on! The oil was the beautiful colour of liquid copper with emerald-green flecks that glowed as brightly in the dark as a bottleful of glow-worms. Malu Paati sold it in little glass bottles with a label which read: 'Wondergro Supersonic Hair Tonic'.

News about Wondergro spread so quickly that film stars and rock musicians started buying it. And when a popular cricketer admitted, in a magazine interview, that he used Wondergro Supersonic Hair Tonic, orders began pouring in so fast that Malu Paati had to give up her job teaching Maths at the local school to go into the hair tonic business full time.

Malu Paati had not been happy with this unexpected turn of events. To begin with, all her mornings were taken up with gathering herbs and buying fresh ingredients for making hair tonic, leaving her with no time for her usual early morning jog on the beach where she ran barefoot in the sand, not in the least slowed down by the vivid jewel-coloured traditional Kanchipuram silk saris she always wore. Besides, all the gathering and brewing meant she never had the time to visit sick friends carrying a hot home-cooked meal for them, or to enter the Scrabble tournament at the local club, or to help a neighbour with elaborate advice. She was greatly respected and well-liked in her town and everyone, from the bus driver's nine-month-old baby to the toothless old lady selling strings of jasmine, called her 'Paati' or 'Grandmother'.

Paati realised that she could no longer run her business by herself. She had to employ an assistant. Once more, it was Veerapandi, the town's champion wrestler, who came to Paati's help. Paati would be doing him a favour, he said, rubbing the back of his enormous neck shyly, if she could keep his only son Damodaran busy every morning.

'Damu attends college only in the evenings,' Veerapandi said. 'Says he's going to become an accountant. But that boy has so much energy, that even after a two-hour workout in my wrestling gym every morning—I make him pound a basket of corn with a wooden pounding stick and run six kilometres carrying the grinding stone—that fellow still has enough energy left to drive his mother crazy at home. It would be a relief if you could use him to help you every morning.'

At first Paati had been most reluctant to take on someone with a tattoo on his shoulder, pink streaks in his long hair (he used Wondergro too) and a shiny gold ring in one ear. But to her surprise, she found Damu hardworking and efficient. Besides, thanks to his boundless energy, Damu could answer the phone, stir the mixture on the stove, grind a batch of Kettletop Nettles and calculate last month's profits on Paati's new computer, all at the same time. Since Damu had started helping her, business was doing better than ever. Best of all, Paati now had time for yoga and jogging and attending Carnatic music concerts.

If only this problem of someone trying to steal her secret formula could be sorted out, Paati sighed. Why would anyone want to steal her secret formula? Were these the 'wrong hands' her father had written about? What or whom had he meant by that? Why had he warned her never to let the formula out of sight? All these questions worried her that morning as she carefully added cucumber curls and slivers of jackfruit seed into the mixture simmering in the heavy iron pan on the stove. As she stirred, she kept checking against the secret formula kept propped up on the coffee pot. She had to make sure that she didn't leave out a single one of the three hundred and sixteen ingredients that went into making Wondergro Supersonic Hair Tonic.

'What worries me even more is this dangerous trip we have to make to Mounashrampur.' Paati massaged her aching wrist and adjusted the white cap she wore over her silver hair when she was working. 'How am I going to keep the formula safe during the journey?'

'Don't worry, Paati,' Damu took the ladle from her and started stirring the mixture himself. 'Remember, the burglars don't even know that you are going to Mounashrampur. They wouldn't know that you have been invited to the conference at the Mouna Baba Herbal Research Laboratory where your father worked. Besides, you are not travelling alone. All of us are coming with you.'

'That's what bothers me even more,' Paati sighed. 'I don't know whether I should be taking you children along. Vikram is only ten and Laila just two years older. And as for you—you might be strong enough to carry two sacks of rice on your back, but you are only eighteen, little more than a child yourself. How will the three of you handle those Singing Grasses in the forest which can make you dizzy with their songs? And the Tarzan Vines which wrap themselves round your waist and swing you around! There are plants in that forest that haven't yet been catalogued by any botanist!'

The flash of Damu's brilliantly white teeth seemed to light up the room for an instant. This was too thrilling for words. He had heard a lot about Mounashrampur from his father who had won the Wrestling Championship held there last year. Appa had told him all about Mouna Baba, the holy man who had taken a vow of silence, and after whom the town was named. He had told Damu about the lumps of prehistoric lava found on the hillside which had amazing magic properties, and the Weather Flowers which changed colour according to the weather. But Veerapandi hadn't mentioned any Tarzan Vines!

'Don't worry about Laila and Viks, Paati,' Damu calmed his boss. 'I'm there to keep an eye on them. And both of them are perfectly capable of looking after themselves. Laila might be no higher than my elbow but she acts like she is some sort of mob boss. She's so bossy that she really reminds me of … er … er … Can you pass me the beaker of calendula crinkles, please.' Damu realised it would not be very polite to tell Paati that Laila was just like her—minus the rimless spectacles and neat silver bun, of course.

'Viks is a smart fellow too,' Damu went on. 'He's the best shot I've seen. He can hit a single grain of dal from a distance of four hundred metres and …'

'With his catapult!' Paati cut in. 'Of what use is a catapult against burglars? Or against the Porcupine Cactus that shoot you with their needle-like thorns if you walk past them?'

'Is that why you asked us to pack long-sleeved shirts and thick jeans? For protection against the cactus?'

'The thick shirts and jeans will be of some help against the cacti. But you need them mainly to ride the wild hill ponies. It's quite tough considering you have to ride them without a saddle and even without reins!'

Damu just couldn't believe his ears. Riding wild ponies! Wow! This trip was going to be more fun than he had imagined. He grinned in delight as he helped Paati lift the heavy pan off the stove, sorted a fresh batch of tarragon teardrops, made two corrections in last month's account statement and emailed a customer about the hair tonic he had despatched, all at the same time.

World Herbologists Conference

'I've never managed to stay on a horse even with a saddle and reins!' Laila sounded horrified. 'How are we supposed to ride wild hill ponies with nothing to sit on or hold on to?'

'Their manes, Laila!' Damu explained with the superior air of one who was better informed. 'Just hang onto their manes very firmly—it's not easy because these manes are very dry and break off in clumps if you tug even a little. Still, if you hold their manes firmly, the wild ponies won't try to throw you off by bucking! Or trying to kick and bite!'

'Sounds fun!' Vikram sounded cheerful. He had every reason to sound happy. Paati had just given him enormous helpings of his two all-time favourites—sticky pineapple halwa and coconut-stuffed pancakes.

Vikram and Laila lived with their parents in Chennai, which was a two-hour drive from the little town where their grandmother lived. Laila was twelve, and had thick eyebrows that went straight across her forehead with no gap over her snub nose. With both their parents working long hours at their jobs, Laila often had to look after her younger brother. She did so many things for him, that she had become very bossy and Vikram had become hopelessly lazy.

Viks, as Vikram was called, was already almost as tall as Laila, with an appetite that was legendary in their neighbourhood. He had won the Idli-Eating Competition held in his colony three years in a row, managing twenty-two idlis last year when his nearest competitor had retired sick after the nineteenth idli! His mother was very worried because Vikram's feet were growing faster than the rest of him and she was already buying his shoes from the adult section of the shoe store.

A friend of their parents had just dropped the two children at their grandmother's home, where they would be spending most of their summer holidays and they were now discussing the trip to Mounashrampur.

Laila was still worried. 'I know it's a terrific honour and all that for you to be invited to demonstrate your Wondergro Supersonic Tonic at the World Herbologists Conference, Paati. But isn't there some easier way of reaching Mounashrampur?'

'Not really. Going on ponies is the only way we can cross the Vankozhimozhi Forest. The forest is the final stretch between the Kashmakash River and Mounashrampur,' Paati explained. 'But you are right, Laila. It is a great honour for me to be showing the world's greatest herbologists how I make Wondergro Supersonic Hair Tonic. That's why we are taking all this.' She waved her hand to indicate the pans and ladles, the strainers, peelers and graters that Damu was packing carefully.

'That article in the magazine did the trick,' Damu explained, 'Not only did Paati's orders for the hair tonic increase ten-fold, but the famous Chinese herbologist, who is the head of the World Herbologists Council, read the article, and wrote to Paati asking her to send samples of Wondergro to the Mouna Labs for testing.'

'Mmm. And also for verifying whether Wondergro actually works. How surprised every one was to receive the sample with my father's name and mine as the chief formulators! Specially Dr Nandini. She was my father's assistant in the Lab and became the chief scientist at Mouna labs after he died. She couldn't believe that my father had worked on this formula so secretively, without telling her or a single other scientist in the lab.' Paati beamed with pride.

'Wow, Paati! I didn't know you were also considered one of the inventors of Wondergro. I thought you had just followed your father's formula. Can we see the formula? Ma told me it was written in Mounabashalu, the ancient language that is never used outside Mounashrampur. She said the monks of Mounashrampur invented the language as some sort of secret code in which to write all their secret herbal formulations.'

Nothing that the children had heard about the secret formula had prepared them for the sheer beauty of it. It looked more like a work of art than a scientific document. Every alphabet started with an artistic squiggle and ended in an

elaborate curl. As she smoothened out the paper
lovingly, Malu Paati told the children how she
had discovered the formula in a file of papers
that the people in her father's laboratory had
parcelled to her some months after his death.
The file had many of her father's important
papers in it.

'Look, these are the illustrations that gave
me a clue about what this formula was all about,'
Malu Paati pointed to two pictures. One was of
a bald man with a sad face. His mouth was turned
down. This was followed by another picture of

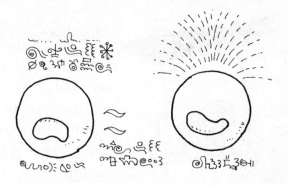

the same man with hair sprouting crazily from the top of his head. In this sketch, the man was smiling happily at the sudden hair bonanza.

'I had a tough time reading the formula,' she went on. 'I hadn't used the language for more than forty years and had almost forgotten it. I couldn't even figure out what some of the ingredients were. Look, here it says, "Add caterpillar footprints to butterfly winks." What could those be?'

'Paati had to change this formula quite a bit. Thank God!' Damu was struggling to tie the vinegar-strainer and pineapple-peeler to the bundle he was packing. 'The original formula insists you have to use "Raisins soaked in camel dung"! Luckily, Paati cut that bit out. Phew! Lucky for me!'

'Yes. Where would you have found camel dung, I wonder,' Laila remarked.

'Paati looks at the formula every time she makes a fresh batch of Wondergro. That's why the paper is so creased. But I haven't looked at the formula for ages. You know, I can remember every single one of the three hundred and sixteen ingredients of Wondergro,' Damu boasted. 'And in the right order. Listen: a drizzle of sea mist, a trickle of honey twists. Six measures of tiger's sighs, 24 scoops of corn eyes. A litre of marigold milk, 3 skeins of snapdragon silk …'

Damu would have gone on and on if Paati hadn't interrupted, 'All that is left for us to do, once Damu finishes packing, is to choose the weapons we need on the trip.'

'Weapons! Will it come to that? Using weapons?' Laila was startled.

'One of the students at Appa's Wrestling Gym

is a Fight Director in the movies. I can get some weapons from him if you want.'

'There's no need for that. I have my own secret store of weapons. But I don't want you to tell anyone about it.' Making the action of her lips being zipped together, Paati led them all to one corner of the room where the ceiling was low. And before their amazed eyes, she pulled down a little rope ladder from the ceiling.

As they looked on in wonder, she nimbly climbed the rope ladder, pushed up a door leading to a loft no one had ever seen before, and disappeared into it.

'What are you waiting for children?' Paati's voice came from the loft. 'Come up here!'

Paati's Secret Weapons

'This looks like Ali Baba's cave!' It was Laila who broke the silence. They had climbed up the rope ladder into a small loft which had just one dusty window letting in a little light. When they stood upright, their heads brushed the roof. Various objects glinted in the dark till Malu Paati switched on a light.

The room was filled with the most interesting objects. A blue silk umbrella with gold tassels and a carved handle. Bronze statues with

glittering green eyes made of some glowing stone. Onyx lamp stands. There were boxes, chests and baskets filled with all sorts of wonderful things. The children rummaged excitedly.

'Look, a chess set with the chess pieces wearing little silk clothes and jewels.'

'My goodness! A harp! I've seen these only in books!'

'Wow! A boomerang!'

'We are here for the weapons. Let's not forget that, children,' Paati reminded them. She looked under the broken lampshades; she pushed aside a wicker basket. 'Now, where could that box of weapons have gone? I have some stuff in it that

21

once belonged to Aruval Varadappa.' The children shivered when Malu Paati mentioned the smuggler who was feared all across the coast for carrying a sickle, or *aruval,* in his belt. 'I also have some items that belonged to Sharp-fingers Oscar. Both of them were my students once. Sharp-fingers was so good at Maths. Just push that rocking horse to one side, Damu! Where could it be?' she muttered as she lifted up a wooden pail used for making ice-cream.

After some time, Malu Paati held up a cardboard box. 'Here! I've found it!'

'That small, dusty, torn, cardboard box has your weapons?' Laila sounded disappointed. She had imagined a slim wooden box long enough to hold a gun. She had pictured herself riding

through the forest with a spear or maybe even a sword. This box didn't look like it could hold a sword or a spear or a gun.

'Whenever I found my students playing with something during class, I took it away from them. At the end of the year, some students would come and take their belongings back, but some would not bother. This carton has a lot of the stuff that I have confiscated from my students over the many years I taught in school.'

Malu Paati opened the carton. In it were things that were even more exciting than the stuff lying in the room. Cricket balls, croquet balls and crazy balls that never stopped bouncing. Catapults of every shape and size. Wooden tops. Little metal clickers, flutes and mouth organs. Yo-yos. Tiny metal soldiers and handmade wooden aeroplanes.

'Now, I want you to choose one weapon each.'

'Paati! These are children's toys. How can we protect ourselves and the secret formula with these?'

'These are no ordinary toys. Look at this length of twine! This twine was once the most prized possession of a student whose family was in the diamondcutting business. You know how children fly kites using *manja,* which is string dipped in ground glass? Well, this boy had lengths of twine dipped in diamond dust. This twine can cut through steel chains. I caught the boy trying it on the lock of the principal's office.'

Laila took the twine and put it in her pocket.

Viks was thrilled to discover a collection of stones. 'It's really difficult to find such perfectly smooth round ones,' he said, slipping a handful into his pocket.

'Is this part of an old gramophone?' Damu held up something which looked like a small horn with a handle.

'Oh, that's what I took away from a group of boys in my first year of teaching. It was the old Tamil master's hearing aid. The boys stole it. Poor man! I couldn't return it to him because he left town soon after. The naughty boys were using it to listen in to conversations in the staff room.'

'Well, a hearing aid won't be much use in Mounashrampur where the people have taken a vow of silence and don't speak at all,' was Viks's comment.

'It's only the Holy Man, the Mouna Baba, and his monks in the ashram who have taken the vow of silence,' Damu said. 'The other people in the town speak quite normally.'

'Well, most of them speak normally,' Paati added with a twinkle. 'When you meet Dr

Nandini, you'll find that she speaks like she has an old, rusted, broken-down siren inserted in her throat where her vocal cords should be—sort of gruff and whiny and extremely loud at the same time. When she calls me on the telephone, I feel I can hear her even without holding the receiver to my ear!'

Everyone laughed and no one paid much attention to Damu slipping the hearing aid into his pocket with a thoughtful look.

'You haven't taken any weapon, Paati! Choose something!' That was Laila taking charge.

'Well, let's see. I think I'll take this animal whistle. The sound it produces can't be heard by humans but the student who owned this whistle would use it to call monkeys into the classroom whenever there was a Maths test. Just seconds after he blew the whistle, the class would be full of monkeys and I would have to postpone the test!' Paati looked wistful as she thought back of those days. How she missed her school and her students!

As they climbed down, their clothes were dusty and their hair was strung with cobwebs.

'We're fully equipped now,' Malu Paati looked satisfied. 'Let's decide who will carry the secret formula. How do we keep it safe on the trip?'

'It's simple,' said Laila. 'The four of us have to share the duty of keeping the formula safe. Right?'

And before anyone could stop her, she had picked up the precious secret paper and torn it into four pieces.

'What are you doing, Laila? Oh my gosh, she's torn the secret formula!' Paati was horrified.

'Now, each of us carries one piece. When we get to Mounashrampur, we stick the pieces together. It's very simple! Don't you think it's a good idea, Paati?'

Paati took the four pieces in her hands, still looking appalled. Her normally calm face had crumpled into hundreds of little worry lines. She thought this was a dreadful idea. The formula would be useless if even one of the pieces was lost.

Then she took several deep breaths and her face became serene once more. She gave her granddaughter a hug and said, 'We won't know if we don't try, will we? Wash your hands and we'll all have some more pineapple halwa!'

Screeching Scientist

'You promised to bring me that formula in a week's time. It has been three weeks now, and you come snivelling to me saying you haven't found it yet!' Dr Nandini Kumar thundered. She was the chief scientist at the Mouna Herbal Research Laboratory and looked like a huge shaggy snowman built in the shape of an American football player—except that she didn't need any shoulder pads to get such broad shoulders!

'You are a nincompoop, Khabardar Khan! A total dimwit!' Dr Nandini's voice was every bit as deafeningly whiny and raspy as Paati had described. 'You are supposed to be the most feared robber in all of Mounashrampur and yet you allow one poor, doddering, old lady to get the better of you! How is it that you have not yet found the secret formula and brought it to me?'

Khabardar Khan looked ashamed. It was true that he was so feared all over Mounashrampur that mothers forced their children to eat by saying 'Khabardar Khan will come and get you if you don't eat your mashed brinjal and boiled yam!'

'It's true that Mrs Malu is old,' Khabardar Khan admitted. 'But she is neither doddering, nor poor, nor a lady! She dives into the sea in her silk sari to collect seaweed for making the hair tonic. She climbs the topmost branches of the tamarind tree in her compound to shake down the raw green tamarind for her tonic. And she's bought herself a new red scooter that she drives faster than any movie stuntman. She is no normal or ordinary old person!'

'I don't care if she climbs a tree or climbs the Eiffel Tower. You bilious bombazine! You curdled crankshaft! You … you … recycled fish-food! I want that paper!'

'But I've already searched every inch of Mrs Malu's house,' Khabardar protested. 'There is no secret formula there! Haven't I already brought you every paper in her house that was written in Mounabashalu?'

'You shoe-with-no-sole! You left-over-soggy-toast! You total idiot! So far, you've brought me: one birth certificate, three letters written to Mrs Malu by her late husband! Yuck! One bill for repairing a water heater and the layout of the sewage pipes. Where's my secret formula?'

'But if you wrote that formula, why can't you just write it again. You must have made notes!'

'You fossilized old vulture! You ossified old fishbone! You petrified old tree stump!' Dr Nandini ranted, 'I want that original formula which is in my handwriting. You think I want the recipe for some silly hair oil? Do I look like I need hair oil?'

Khabardar Khan had to admit that Dr Nandini didn't seem in the need of hair oil. Her bushy eyebrows looked like two enormous white bottle-brushes. She had white hair growing out of her ears and nose, and from her knuckles and toes. She even had something of a moustache!

'Why did you write a formula for hair tonic

if you didn't need it?' Khabardar Khan looked puzzled as he scratched the huge black mole at the tip of his nose out of which grew three long hairs.

'You pea-brain! You fused bulb! You mouldy machine! That's not a formula for hair tonic. It's something more powerful! It's ... well ... I can't tell you. But if that paper gets into the wrong hands, I may even have to go to prison! That goody-goody-dumpling ... that Mouna Baba. How I hate him! Ever since he was chosen to take over the ashram from the Mouna Baba before him, it's been a problem for me. Checks

our accounts like we were schoolchildren. Has cut down our expenses by more than half! It's so unfair! Anyway, I want that formula NOW! NOW!!!'

'But isn't Mrs Malu bringing the formula here when she comes for the World Herbologists Conference in a few days? I can easily get it for you when she's in Mounashrampur.'

'You pie-faced piranha! You tarantula with toe-jam! You hippopotamus with halitosis! That paper has to be in my hands before this crazy

tree-climbing, sea-diving Malu arrives in Mounashrampur. Here, every one reads Mounabashalu and will realise that the paper does not have a formula for making hair tonic! I do not want the formula to reach here. If it wasn't for that over-enthusiastic, hyper-zealous Chinese herbologist writing to Malu and inviting her for the World Herbologists Conference, no one would have ever known about the formula.'

In spite of all the explanations, there was still one question which bothered Khabardar Khan. 'Why did you give the old lady the secret formula if it was so dangerous?'

'You dusty dumbbell! You cobwebbed coat-hanger! I didn't give the formula to her. I pushed it into a file lying on my desk when someone walked into my room. I had to leave my room for a second and when I returned, the file was missing. My secretary, who is a bigger nitwit than you are, had already parcelled the file, along with the secret formula, to Malu. It was a file of her father's personal papers. That's how that old crow Malu got hold of it. She's read it all wrong and made a hair tonic from the formula for making a deadly … er … well from my secret formula. I need that secret formula before Malu and her brats reach Mounashrampur. This is your last chance, Khabardar Khan!'

Khabardar Khan knew Dr Nandini was perfectly serious. He had to get the secret formula somehow. He knew that Malu Paati, her assistant and her two grandchildren were starting out on the journey to Mounashrampur soon. They would be carrying the formula with them.

It would be easier once they got on the boat. The boatman owed him a favour and would agree to help. The most-feared burglar knew he needed all the help possible if he was to get his hands on the secret formula.

The Beginning of a Long Journey

Damu's father, Veerapandi, drove Paati and the three children to the bus stop in his own auto. He supported his family by driving an auto whenever he wasn't wrestling or teaching wrestling or taking part in a wrestling match.

'Damu's mother has packed a small, simple breakfast for you,' he told Paati shyly, handing over a bag which looked large enough to transport a refrigerator. Damu's mother's idea of a small, simple breakfast for four people consisted of several dozen boiled eggs, piles of puris with spicy potato, and an enormous bunch of bananas from their own tree.

All through the drive, Veerapandi kept shouting bits of advice to Damu over the loud sputtering of his auto.

'Don't forget to give the gift to Chanchanachan when you meet him! And try bringing me a lump of magic lava. You can find it on the river bed. Or under the pine needles fallen on the hillside. Or …'

'We have to get onto the bus now,' Paati broke in. 'Count all the pieces of luggage! One, two, three, four … we had eight pieces between the four of us … five, six … which includes the two bags with the vessels and all the herbs. Make sure we've unloaded all the bags from the auto

'… seven, eight. Yes, all the bags are here.'

The last bag was put into the bus and they all clambered in. The bus took off with a jolt that sent many people sprawling.

'Who is this person you are carrying a gift for?' Laila asked Damu.

'Oh, that's Chanchanachan. My father is so grateful to him. You know my father won the Wrestling Championship held at Mounashrampur last year. It was his first win in four years. It was something of a miraculous victory …'

'Listen to this story, Viks,' Laila interrupted to call her brother over. Viks suffered from motion sickness and was already beginning to look a bit green. He needed to be distracted or else he would end up feeling very ill indeed.

'Last year, Appa bought himself an air-ticket to Mounashrampur,' Damu continued, 'because it was far quicker and much cheaper than going by bus, then by boat, then by pony, like we are. His journey by air would take him to Mounashrampur from the other side! That's the side of the hill that even the ponies can't climb.

'When Appa reached the top of the cliff, he realised why the air-ticket had been so cheap. There was a long, lo-o-o-ng platform jutting over the cliff. The air-ticket covered the rental for a parachute. You strap on the parachute, walk to the end of the platform and jump off. That's the air-trip to Mounashrampur!'

Viks's motion sickness improved dramatically on hearing the story.

'Appa was wearing a lungi, so when he parachuted off the cliff, he lost his wallet with all his money. His lungi flew off too and he also lost his bag of clothes somewhere mid-air! Worst of all, he lost the precious bit of magic lava that had been in his family for years. That bit of lava could magically heal sprained muscles, torn ligaments and other injuries that wrestlers often get. Just by being placed on the injured part! Anyway ... when Appa landed safely on the stretch cleared for the parachuters, he had no money, no change of clothes—nothing.'

The scene he described was so funny and the kids laughed so much that Paati made Damu repeat the entire story.

'This clearing where Appa landed is just outside Mouna Baba's ashram—it's called Mouna Ashram. Which means "Silent Abode". All the monks and holy men in the ashram are totally silent. The only ones allowed to speak in the ashram are the special group of kalari monks. Those are the warrior monks who act as guards.

All the food for the ashram is supplied from a kitchen which is run by Chanchanachan.

'Chanchanachan helped Appa by employing him for a few days. Appa would carry the fruit, milk and sweets up to all the rooms. In return for the work, Appa was allowed to eat and drink as much fruit, sweet and milk as he wanted. He had no money and he would have starved if he hadn't met Chanchanachan. And he couldn't have won the Wrestling Championship either. That's why Appa is sending him a gift.'

By this time, the bus had reached the river bank. Looking out of the window, they could see the Kashmakash River. The muddy waters were churning as wildly as cold-coffee in a blender. Laila felt really worried. The little boats were saucer-shaped and made of cane and buffalo hide.

'Count the bags. We must unload eight bags,' Paati ordered. 'One, two …'

'But Paati that's the bag with the breakfast Damu's mother made for us. So there must be nine bags in all. Not just the eight we started off with.' That was Laila, being responsible as usual.

Everyone stopped in their tracks. Oh no! They had left one bag behind in Veerapandi's auto.

When he realised what had happened, Viks looked more sick than ever. It was his backpack that had been left behind in the auto. Worse still, his piece of secret formula was in that backpack! This was not the best time to tell everyone about this missing bit of formula, he decided. Not when they were all looking so anxiously at the flimsy boat.

The saucer-shaped boat bobbed frighteningly when they all stepped in.

'Ready to leave?' asked the boatman. The huge black mole at the tip of his nose had three long hairs growing out of it.

Across the River Kashmakash

The dark churning waters of the Kashmakash river tossed the boat around like a feather in the wind. Poor Vikram! The rocking of the boat was making him turn the same shade as the boatman's corduroy trousers—bright-green!

Paati felt uneasy as she watched the boatman. He had a belly so big that it seemed like he'd stuffed a sack of potatoes into his tight, yellow T-shirt. Worse still, the clumsy fellow had almost dropped the oar into the river twice. What a disaster that would have been! This type of boat used just one oar, and without it, the boat would be at the mercy of the wildly whirling waters.

'Watch out!' Paati shouted out to the boatman, 'That's the third time you've almost dropped the oar into the water. What's the matter? You're behaving like you've never rowed a boat before!'

The boatman grinned nastily, then quickly hid the flash of blackened teeth behind fingers the size of small bananas. Had the old lady somehow guessed the truth, he wondered. For he was no regular boatman. He was Khabardar Khan and this was the first time he had ever held an oar in his hands. His evil plan was going well, Khabardar thought proudly when he heard the sound he had been waiting for ever since this boat had left the shore. The loud purr of a motor boat.

Paati and the children watched the motor boat heading in their direction. To their surprise, the man driving the motor boat waved out cheerfully and shouted out, 'Oy! I'm here Khabardar Bhai. You can start your operation! I'm here!'

'What's going on, Mr ... er ... Mr Khabardar? Who is this man? What on earth are you doing with your nose to the floor of the boat instead of rowing?' Paati had to address her questions to the boatman's bright-green corduroy bottom

because he had bent over and
was fiddling with something at the base of the
boat.

When Khabardar finally stood up, laughing
wildly and wickedly, he was waving something
that looked like a big, black, rubber bullet. It
was a bit of rubber that fit snugly into the hole
that he had drilled at the bottom of the boat
earlier.

Paati and the children stared at him in shock.
They knew something dreadful was happening
but couldn't figure out what. Not till they heard
the water gurgling into the boat through the hole
and felt their ankles getting wet.

Then everything seemed to happen all at once. Paati shouted and Laila screamed while poor Viks just quietly turned a brighter shade of green! Damu lunged for Khabardar's hand trying to pull the rubber plug from him. The boat rocked crazily and the screaming grew louder. Khabardar laughed and tossed the rubber plug into the water.

By now, the motor boat had sputtered to a halt right next to their little boat so that Khabardar just had to step from one boat to the other. But before he left the little boat, Khabardar picked up the single oar and flung it into the water like a spear.

'There!' he said spitefully, 'Now, you can all drown! You can drown along with your precious secret formula!' His evil laugh rang in their ears as the motor boat zoomed off.

'Secret formula?' Paati was in a daze. 'Is he talking about my secret formula for making Wondergro Supersonic Hair Tonic?'

'He must have been the person trying to steal your formula all along. That fat man, the one called Khabardar,' Laila pointed out. 'And now he wants to sink our boat and destroy the formula forever!'

'Don't worry about the formula now! He wants to destroy us! Think of what we should do next,'

Damu didn't take his eyes off his feet. Both of them were planted firmly over the hole in the boat but the water just trickled steadily in.

Could they swim, he wondered. He knew Paati was a good swimmer and went diving for seaweed regularly. But could Viks and Laila manage?

'Swimming is out of the question,' Paati seemed to read his thoughts. 'We can't even see the shore from here. Besides, this river has currents more deadly than the sea. And there is a waterfall further down that we can get swept into.'

The tense silence that followed was broken by a most surprising sound. The clinking sound of the pots and pans they were carrying with them. Even more surprising was the fact that it was Viks who was doing the unpacking! He had undone the bundle and now stood with a boiled egg in one hand and a pan in the other.

'Hole! Water!' was all he

could manage to croak as he swayed greenly.

'He means plug the hole with the egg and bail the water out with the pan,' Laila explained, a hopeful grin lighting up her face. Could they do it?

They all got into action. Finding that the boiled egg didn't block the hole properly, Damu wrapped it in several layers of the green plantain leaf in which their breakfast had been wrapped. The leaf was waterproof and now the boiled egg stayed firmly in place. The water stopped trickling in.

Laila and Viks chose the largest pots and scooped the water out of the boat. Laila's arms moved so fast that she looked like a human windmill while Viks moved just enough to convince any onlooker that he was not a green marble statue. In no time at all, most of the water was poured back into the river and the boat was bobbing merrily again.

Paati, in the meantime, had taken one of the long ladles that Damu had packed and was trying to row the boat. The ladle was so much shorter than the oar that they managed to move forward just a fraction each time she rowed.

Damu took his turn with the ladle next. Then Laila did. Viks, exhausted with all this unexpected activity, said that he was feeling too sick to row. Slowly, bit by bit, they made their way to the river bank.

Their arms were aching when they unloaded their bags on to dry land.

Paati hugged the children in relief. 'Good job, children. We've crossed the Kashmakash river. We've reached the shores of the Vankozhimozhi Forest. Now, if we manage to catch those wild ponies and ride them across the forest, we will reach Mounashrampur. Look, there they are!'

Their first look at the ponies made the children's hearts sink. They were small ponies. No bigger than the donkey their dhobi used, to carry his bundles of washing. But the wild ponies had large, yellow, front teeth that made grinding sounds as they chewed the sweet starburst flowers and the juicy moonshadow vines. And as they watched the group of humans suspiciously, the ponies pawed the ground and sometimes even nibbled each others' tails and ears in a manner that did not seem entirely friendly.

'Catch those ponies!' Laila sounded doubtful. 'I think it would be easier to extract a crocodile's tooth!'

'It would even be simpler to wrestle with a

bear like my grandfather used to,' Damu didn't seem confident either.

But Viks smiled. 'The animal whistle!' he guessed. 'That's why you picked the animal whistle from the box, isn't it, Paati? So that you could call the ponies easily?'

'Smart boy,' Paati took the whistle out of a small silk pouch she wore at her waist. 'The animal-calling whistle is part of my plan. But the most important of all, is this.'

In her hand, she held a small glass bottle filled with something that looked like melted chocolate!

Singing Grasses and Tarzan Vines

The Vankozhimozhi Forest was full of the most amazing sights. Once Paati and the children had mastered the art of staying on the wild ponies, they were able to admire the colourful mushrooms as large as garden umbrellas, the flowers which looked like translucent balloons and the bushes doubling over with the weight of juicy berries in shades of purple, blue and red.

Staying on the ponies, with their entire luggage

strapped on to their backs, was not an easy job. Without reins and saddles, Paati and the children seemed in danger of sliding off with every bumpy step.

'You are a genius, Paati. Your idea of making a concentrated version of Wondergro Supersonic Hair Tonic to apply to the ponies' manes was absolutely brilliant!' Damu wished he had thought of the idea himself. 'Now that the manes are well oiled, they won't break at the slightest tug. That would be disastrous, wouldn't it?'

'Yes, if you loosen your grip on their manes, just because chunks of it break off in your hands, you could end up flat on your nose in a bed of poison ivy or get thrown up on a tree right next to a hive of Behemoth Bees that could sting you to death. This forest is a dangerous place,' Paati warned them. 'I made a concentrated version of Wondergro so that I could carry it in one tiny bottle small enough to be tucked into the purse at my waist.

It's extremely concentrated. That's why it looks like dark chocolate. I had to use just a few drops on each pony. Look, the bottle is still almost full.'

'If you ask me, this concentrated version makes hair grow at a real supersonic speed,' Viks insisted. 'I think my pony's mane is longer already. When we started off, I could barely cling on and now, look—aaargh!' He broke off as his pony suddenly bucked, pawed the air with its front legs, kicked up its hind legs like a donkey and settled down with a thump that made Viks's teeth rattle.

'Hang on tight, Viks. Don't worry, children, it's not much longer to Mounashrampur.' Paati looked around her. This bit of the forest was familiar to her. 'After we get through this clump of trees, we come to the most dangerous bit of our journey. We have the Singing Grasses to the right of us and the Porcupine Cacti to the left of us. The Singing Grasses are less dangerous because you can drown their humming by either speaking or singing loudly. I've always found it best to recite something that will keep you alert, like the multiplication tables. That way, we won't … shhh … wait a minute.' Paati stopped talking and listened. They could hear a low growling sound.

'I'm quite sure there are no wild animals here. What could that sound be?'

'Oh my gosh, Paati, look! It's those two jelly-bellies. Those two tabla-tummies! Those wicked men who tried to sink us! That boatman called Khabardar and the man in the motor boat,' Laila said.

Paati and the children were peering through the snake-shaped creepers that dropped down from the trees like a curtain across their path.

Yes, it was Khabardar Khan and the man in the motor boat! They lay on the long grass, fast asleep, their mouths wide open as they snored! How had these wicked villains got here, Paati wondered, feeling her eyelids drooping. She yawned, beginning to feel rather drowsy.

Then she shook herself awake sternly. This sleepiness was just the effect of the dreaded Singing Grasses of the Vankozhimozhi Forest. The two villains had probably made the mistake of riding through the grasses, felt sleepy, and been thrown off their ponies, right into the middle of the Singing Grasses. That's why they were still fast asleep.

'Seven ones are seven. Seven twos are fourteen,' Damu shouted loudly when he realised that Paati was feeling sleepy. 'Don't let the Singing

Grasses get to you, Paati. Come on, Viks and Laila,' he urged, 'start speaking or singing loudly.'

Viks, who could never remember his multiplication tables, burst into a horribly tuneless 'Baa Baa Black Sheep' with such unexpected loudness that his pony was startled into shooting off at a fast trot. This distracted Paati in the middle of her 'eight eights are ...' so she didn't hear a whooshing sound. She didn't hear Laila and Damu yell, 'Watch out, Paati! That looks like a Tarzan Vine.'

Suddenly, she felt herself being clasped around the waist, lifted right off her pony, whizzed through the air and finally released with a soft thud right on to something which felt as springy and spongy as a water bed!

When she scrambled up in a daze, she realised she had been carried by the Tarzan Vine and thrown right on to the sleeping

Khabardar Khan.

Khabardar was jolted awake.

'Aaieeeeek!' he shrieked, his face turning white in terror. 'The old woman! I drowned her! She has returned as a ghost to haunt me! Heeelllp!! Gho-o-o-st!'

The man who had been driving the motor boat woke up and joined the yelling.

'Nine twos are eighteen, nine threes are twenty-seven,' Paati shouted. The humming was so much louder right in the middle of the grasses that she had to yell at the top of her voice!

'Eeeek! Help. This ghostly witch is chanting mantras and spells at us. Where's my bag? I have a gun!'

The word 'gun' stirred Paati to action. She fumbled in the silk purse at her waist for the only weapon she had with her. The bottle of concentrated Wondergro Supersonic Hair Tonic! She removed the little cork stopper and flung the thick liquid on to their faces.

'Yaaargh! Oowooch! Kreeegah!' The men screamed in surprise. Paati dashed off without stopping to look back at the two men trying to rub the chocolate-coloured liquid off their faces!

The children were waiting for her on the narrow path between the Porcupine Cacti and the Singing Grasses. Laila and Damu were tiredly chanting the multiplication tables as loudly as their parched throats would allow while Viks was still singing 'Baa Baa Black Sheep' in a dull tuneless manner.

And waiting with the children was a whole new set of problems to be sorted out. There were no ponies in sight. The children had obviously been thrown off by the ponies which had then run away. They now sat crouched on the path, with different bits of clothing wrapped around their heads and arms as protection. Paati

felt a scorpion-like sting on her arm as she reached the group.

'Oouch,' she winced in pain as she removed the thorn which the Porcupine Cacti had shot into her arm. How were they going to get through this part of the forest without getting a thorn up their noses, or even worse, through their eyes, she wondered. How were they going to get to Mounashrampur without the ponies?

Paati refused to walk through the Singing Grasses again.

'Those villains have a gun,' she explained. 'We can't take the risk of going near them. We'll just have to go through the Porcupine Cacti somehow.'

Damu's shoulders were aching. He looked thin and wiry but was, in fact, extremely strong. When he trained at his father's wrestling gym every morning, he used two fifty-kilo sacks of rice instead of dumbbells. So he had been given the heaviest bundles to carry. He eased the bag off his shoulders, letting it drop to the ground with a clang that sent the pomegranate-seeder, the ginger-grater and the spinach-oil strainer spinning on to the soft grass.

Paati picked up the spinach-oil strainer. She held it over her face and her smile beamed right through the steel mesh at the children. 'Who would have thought we'd be carrying masks and helmets with us!' was her only comment as she started searching the bundle.

'Hold that over your face like this as we go through the cacti,' she said handing Viks the big strainer. 'And here's a strainer for you, Laila. You can use this grater, Damu. I'll manage with the cane basket over my head.'

And so, swathed in layers of clothing, wearing the pots and baskets over their heads like helmets, holding the strainers over their faces like masks and looking like characters from some Bronze Age action thriller, Paati and the children got safely past the Porcupine Cacti.

The Missing Piece

Their first sight of Mounashrampur made the children gasp in delight. The little town looked like someone had taken every single colour out of a jumbo box of crayons and used it to paint the town. Each door, window and window-pane of every single house was painted in a different colour. The air smelt of freshly-squeezed lemon.

'It's not much further to Mouna Labs,' Paati comforted the children who were grumbling about having to walk some more. 'Just think of something pleasant as you walk.'

'The only thing that's keeping me going is the pleasant thought of taking back a lump of magic lava for my father, to replace the lucky one he lost! I'll have to look under the fallen pine needles as we walk up the hill,' Damu sighed tiredly.

The road ahead was very steep. Even Paati, who had sprinted through the Vankozhimozhi Forest without being in the least out of breath, was breathing noisily by the time they reached the tall iron gates of Mouna Herbal Research Laboratory. Hung over the gate was a colourful banner welcoming scientists to the World Herbologists Conference which was starting the next day. The security guard at the gate peered suspiciously at them.

'We are here for the World Herbologists Conference,' Paati panted.

The guard let them in after using the telephone to check with Nandini. There was another long walk from the gate to the smart, glass-fronted building. Through the enormous glass doors, Paati and the children could see people waiting for them.

'See! People waiting to welcome us,' Paati seemed to revive with the excitement.

'But they don't seem very friendly,' Viks screwed up his eyes and stared hard. 'In fact, they look like they're holding ... oh my gosh ... they look like they're holding guns!'

The glass doors burst open and four guards came charging towards them. They grabbed Malu Paati and the children and started pushing them roughly inside the building.

'Take your hands off the children at once. How dare you push me like this?' Paati spoke sternly, but it had no effect on the guards who forced them into one of the rooms.

Inside the room, behind a polished desk, sat a lady with two braids of frizzy white hair which stuck out from her head at the oddest possible angles. Next to the desk, stood an elderly gentleman dressed in a white dhoti and kurta. He had a black patch over one eye. There was something commanding, even a little frightening, about this old man. Paati couldn't remember having ever met him at Mouna Labs when her father had been alive.

'Dr Nandini,' Paati turned to the lady in relief, 'thank God you are here. We are safe now, children. Dr Nandini will take care of everything!'

'I should have taken care of you many months ago,' Dr Nandini snarled. 'That useless Khabardar

Khan. That lopsided liver cutlet! He telephoned me feeling very pleased with himself to tell me that the four of you were lying at the bottom of the river along with the secret formula. And now I find you are here! All four of you! It's the very thing I wanted to avoid at all costs!'

'Avoid at all costs?' Paati was puzzled. 'But why? You were the one who asked us to come a day earlier than all the other scientists and herbologists invited for the conference. You wanted to see the formula for yourself before anyone at the conference saw it! And now you say that you wanted to avoid our visit at all costs! Why?'

'I never thought you would actually succeed in reaching here along with the secret formula, you … you … you foolish falooda, you slimy spaghetti with mildewed meatballs, you moronic murukku!' Nandini's voice rose with every phrase she uttered. 'Khabardar was supposed to steal the formula from you. He was supposed to make sure you didn't bring the formula here. Now hand over the formula to me. At once!'

'Certainly not!' The look of bewilderment on Malu Paati's face was replaced by anger. 'I absolutely refuse to hand over the formula to you!'

'Guards!' Nandini snapped her fingers. The guards surrounded the group and there was an ominous clicking of guns.

Paati looked at the three children. She would never put Laila, Vikram and Damu at any risk. She quickly took her piece of the formula out of the locket she was wearing round her neck and handed it over.

'Why has this formula been torn? Where's the rest of it, you ingrown toenail! You villainous vermiform appendix!' Nandini thundered when she looked at the piece she had been given.

She calmed down a little when Laila handed over her piece of formula. Laila had hidden it inside the cavity of her rubber doll's body and had to unscrew her doll's head to get it.

Reluctantly, Damu reached into his bag and took out a tin of talcum powder. 'I need a tin-opener to get to the formula. I just made a slit in the top of this tin and slid the formula in.'

'Do you think this is a kitchen? Where will I get a tin-opener here?' Nandini shrieked.

'There's no need for a tin-opener, Nandu!' the old man with the black eye-patch spoke for the first time. From the pocket of his kurta, he pulled out a small gun. Ignoring the gasps of fright from Paati and the children, the old man put the tin on the floor in one corner of the room and fired a shot through it.

The tin exploded in a puff of white dust. Out came the third piece of the formula, smelling sweet, coated with white powder and with a neat hole in the centre of the paper where the bullet had gone through it!

Paati and the children were quite scared now! These were dangerous people. They were prepared to go to any lengths to get their hands

on the secret formula. The three pieces of the formula were now placed on the desk like a jigsaw puzzle.

'Oh no! The most important piece is missing,' Nandini's eyes blazed in fury, 'The one with the diagram and the actual chemical composition. And the explanation of how it works.'

'You mean the sketch of the bald man looking sad and then looking happy when he starts sprouting hair?' Paati asked. 'That's what got me working on the formula. I don't read Mounabashalu too well and ...'

'That's not a sketch of a bald man you ... you gust of bad-breath, you ... you fumes from the sewer,' Nandini snorted. 'That's a sketch of a ...'

'Enough, Nandu!' the man with the black eye-patch interrupted. 'There's no need for these people to know more than they should.'

'Why Appa? These people are going to be history soon. And part of geography too. Filling a space six feet under the ground on the slopes of Mounashrampur.'

'Don't be ridiculous, Nandu. Once we have the last piece of the formula, there will be no need to kill these blundering fools. They know nothing. I will burn the entire paper so that nothing can be traced back to us. Especially since we are trying the operation again today. We cannot have it falling into the wrong hands!'

Paati suddenly had a thoughtful look on her face.

'You are Nandini's father. And you call your daughter "Nandu",' she mused aloud, looking at the man. 'You say you don't want the paper to "fall into the wrong hands". So *you* were the one who scribbled that note on the formula that I have! The note that read, "Don't let this paper out of your sight. Can't have it falling into the wrong hands." The writing was so shaky that I read it wrong. That note was actually meant for *"Nandu"*, but I thought it was for me—*"Malu"*. But why do you want my father's secret formula for making hair oil?'

'Quiet! Here we ask the questions?'

'Your turn now, boy!' Nandini ignored Paati and looked under her bushy brows at Vikram.

'I can't give you my piece,' Vikram sounded desperate.

The stunned silence that followed his statement was broken by a series of ominous clicks as the guards pointed their guns at him.

'Don't be a hero. Give her your piece, Vikram,' Laila commanded.

'Give her your piece of the formula!' ordered Paati and Damu together.

'I can't,' Viks looked miserable and frightened. 'My piece of formula is in my comic … which is in my backpack … which I left in the auto … Veerapandi mama's auto.'

Chanchanachan and the Laddoo Express

Dr Nandini was yelling loud enough to be heard all the way up to Veerapandi's Wrestling Gymnasium even without the telephone.

'I don't care if he is in a wrestling match. Give your boss Veerapandi my message immediately! Tell him that his snooping son Damu, along with Mrs Meddlesome Malu and her two nosy grandchildren are being held prisoners at the Mouna Labs in Mounashrampur. They will not be harmed if Veerapandi brings the piece of paper kept in a backpack belonging to Vikram. Vikram left the backpack in Veerapandi's auto. It has a picture of a la … er … I mean a bald man on it. The children and the old lady will be set free, unharmed, the minute we have the paper in hand.' She slammed the phone down and glared at her prisoners.

'Take them to the room next door,' Nandini's father ordered the guards.

'At once, Periyaswami *saar*!' The guards leapt to obey him.

'Leave all your bags here,' Nandini's father, Periyaswami, spoke harshly as Damu bent to pick up his bag.

The guards shoved Paati and the children roughly into another room.

'You can try screaming for help if you want,' Periyaswami sniggered nastily before the door closed. 'That room is soundproof.'

The room they were pushed into had no furniture at all. There were heavy bars across the windows. The thick glass was permanently fixed so that the windows could not be opened.

Paati sat on the floor tiredly. Viks and Laila flopped down next to her while Damu paced up

and down for a few
minutes restlessly before putting
his ear to the heavy wooden door.
Then remembering something, he put
his hand into his pocket and took out the
Tamil master's funnel-shaped hearing aid that
he had taken from the box in Paati's house. He
held the broad end to the door and put the narrow
end to his ear.

'It works!' Damu's face lit up. 'Shhh!' He
listened some more and then told them what he
had heard. 'They are planning some operation
today. Where there is a saffron-dipped cashew
nut involved. Oh … this time this cashew nut is
going to be bright orange, dipped in orange food
colouring instead so that it can be seen clearly.
If the plan fails again today, they will have to
wait a whole year to try again.'

He eavesdropped again intently and a worried
look came over his face before he spoke, 'This
is strange. The last time they tried the plan,

somebody ate the saffron-dipped cashew nut instead of giving it to the Mouna Baba. So the plan didn't work. I think they're trying to poison somebody with a bright orange cashew nut. Oh no, it sounds like the Mouna Baba is their target. We have to warn him. But how do we get out of here?'

'We can't get out of here!' Paati looked defeated. 'Look at those heavy bars and the thick glass. And here we are, with nothing to cut the bars or break the glass with!'

'That's not really true,' said Laila. She was looking thoughtfully at the length of twine she had taken out of her pocket. It was the twine dipped in diamond dust that Paati's student had used to cut locks. 'I wonder whether this will work on these bars.'

Excited at the possibility, the children wrapped the length of twine around one of the bars. It wasn't easy. Damu tried pulling the two ends of the twine together and managed to cut his hand. Laila watched seriously and tried another method. She moved the twine like a flexible saw and managed to cut through one bar. It was quite magical to watch. A humble piece of twine cutting a heavy iron bar like a hot knife slicing through butter.

'Yipeee!' Viks shouted.

'Shhhh,' Damu calmed him down, 'it's a good thing this room is soundproof. It means the villains next door can't hear what we are doing.'

'Is that so? Good! Then I know exactly how we can break the glass without cutting ourselves.'

'How, Vikram?'

'I just need something to mark a spot on the glass. I'll get to work after Laila has cut the bars.' Viks tried to figure out what he could use to mark a spot on the glass. They didn't have a pen or chalk.

Laila and Damu had realised that they needed to cut only one end of each bar. After one end had been cut, they could twist the bar upwards to leave a clear opening that they could squeeze through once the glass had been broken. Every time Laila cut a bar with the twine, Damu would bend it upwards with the airy comment, 'This is so much easier than some of the stuff Appa makes me do at the gym.'

Finally, three of the bars had been cut at one end and pushed out of the way. Viks, meanwhile, had been wondering how he could mark a spot on the window. Paati solved the problem. She ran the tips of her fingers through her well-oiled hair and then made little circular movements on the glass with her greasy fingers.

'That's perfect, Paati!' Viks grinned, seeing the greasy spot on the glass. He took his catapult and one of the perfectly smooth stones he had taken from Patti's box, out of his pocket. He aimed carefully and the stone hit the greasy spot on the glass with a sharp smack.

'The secret is to hit the exact same spot with the stone. Hard! Only a really skilled marksman can do it.' He frowned in concentration as he took aim again.

He managed to hit the oily circle with amazing accuracy several times till at last, a crack appeared in the glass. After a few more hits, the single crack turned into a huge cobweb of several cracks. Damu took off his shirt, wrapped it around his fist and managed to knock a large hole in the glass.

'Do you think you can go through that without cutting yourself, Paati?' Viks asked, eyeing the opening they had created. 'Or should we get Laila to cut off one of these bars so we can use it to smash a larger opening.'

Paati just raised an eyebrow in reply. In no time at all, the four of them had climbed out of the window and were making their way behind the bushes. They tiptoed behind a stone building,

past the cycle shed, to a gate just small enough for people to walk through. It was one of the back entrances to Mouna Labs, and there was no guard. Nor was the gate kept locked.

As luck would have it, a small, brightly painted cart stood outside this gate. It was a handcart with two large wheels. Painted on the side of the cart were the words 'Chanchanachan Laddoo Express'.

'Hey, get away from the cart. What are you doing?' came a gruff voice and a man appeared near them. He was as plump and round as a laddoo himself and his shiny, rosy cheeks looked

like he had stuffed several laddoos into his mouth at the same time. But he seemed annoyed. 'Don't hang around here expecting laddoos,' he scolded them. 'This entire lot is being delivered to the Mouna Baba and his monks at the ashram. Laddoos are Mouna Baba's favourite sweet!'

'Are you Chanchanachan, sir?' Damu asked excitedly. 'My father Veerapandi, the famous wrestler, has sent a gift for you.'

'Veerapandi!' the man sounded shocked. 'You mean that enormous giant of a man who was here for the wrestling championships last year? Is he alright? I thought something terrible might have happened to him after he ate the …' He clapped his hand over his mouth and looked guilty.

'Oh-ho, what rubbish I'm talking! Here, laddoos for all of you.' He seemed to have suddenly changed his mind about not giving them sweets. He beamed as he handed out laddoos to all of them, and said with a small bow, 'Yes, I'm Chanchanachan. Sole supplier of fruits and sweets to the Mouna Ashram. How nice to meet you all. So you are Veerapandi's son. Hope you are as strong as your father. Please help me push this cart to Mouna Ashram. Today's the day I need plenty of help to carry the laddoos into the ashram. And in return for your efforts, I will take you for a special private meeting with the Mouna Baba.'

Now that their problem of how to meet the Mouna Baba had been solved, even Viks felt enthused enough to lay his hand lightly on the cart while Laila and Damu pushed energetically. The cart was surprisingly heavy and the wheels wobbled alarmingly over the potholes. But the endless supply of delicious laddoos kept them going up and down the steep slopes leading to Mouna Baba's ashram—the famous Mouna Ashram.

Mouna Baba

'Why are there so many people waiting here?'
Paati whispered, seeing the huge crowd waiting
in the courtyard of the Mouna Ashram.

'Don't you know? Today is the most special
day of the entire year. Mouna Baba meets his
devotees once a year, only on this day. People
have come from all over the world to meet him.
I will take you to meet him in his room. I am one
of the chosen few people allowed into Mouna
Baba's private quarters. I always carry the fruits

and sweets for him,' Chanchanachan boasted.

They stopped outside an enormous door carved with many tiny panels.

'Those are the carved images of the twenty-three previous Mouna Babas who have lived in this ashram. When this Mouna Baba turns sixty, a new Mouna Baba will be chosen to take his place,' Chanchanachan explained.

He pushed the door open and they entered a room that looked like the entrance lobby to a larger hall.

'This is where we prepare everything,' Chanchanachan pointed to the cane baskets, trays and a large silver jug. He arranged the fruits in the basket and piled the laddoos carefully in a pyramid on the tray. He indicated that Paati and Damu should carry the fruits and milk, while he would carry the laddoos himself.

They stepped into a large room with cool marble floors. At the far end of the room, on a simple wooden platform, was a monk dressed in sky-blue robes. His eyes were closed in meditation, he was in the cross-legged 'lotus pose', and he was actually floating a few inches above the platform. From the way everyone in the room gazed at him adoringly, Paati and the children guessed that the levitating monk was

Mouna Baba.

'We have to wait till he opens his eyes,' Chanchanachan whispered.

There was a feeling of absolute peace in the room. Suddenly, Damu's eyes fell on the laddoo placed right at the top of the pyramid arranged carefully by Chanchanachan. Most of the laddoos had cashew nuts on them. But the cashew nut on the topmost laddoo was a bright orange colour!

'Look at the top laddoo,' Damu hissed to Viks. 'It has the poisoned cashew nut on it. The bright orange cashew nut.'

At that moment, Mouna Baba opened his eyes and Chanchanachan started walking towards him with the tray of laddoos in his hands. He motioned for the children and Paati to follow.

'Use your catapult to smash the top laddoo!' Damu's voice was urgent. 'The one with the orange cashewnut! That's the poisoned laddoo! Quick!' Chanchanachan was already halfway across the long hall, far ahead of Laila and Paati, when Viks took his catapult out of his pocket and hurriedly took aim. A moving target was never easy to hit. The angle was all wrong too. Would he be able to hit the laddoo?

Just as he took aim, one of the monks noticed Viks. The monk's eyes widened in alarm and he rushed to ring the huge copper bell placed near the platform. Chanchanachan turned to see what was happening. And just as he turned around, the stone left the catapult, whizzed halfway across the room and hit the topmost laddoo right in the

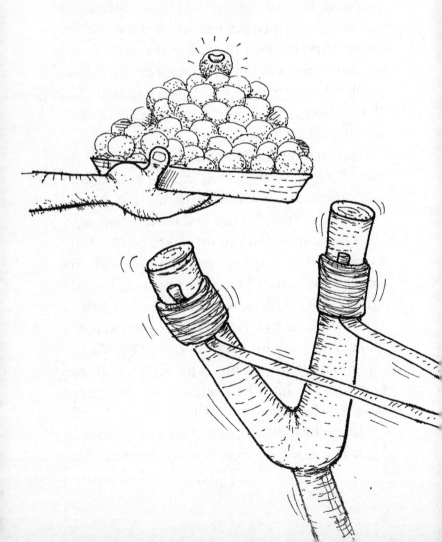

centre with a hard smack. The laddoo smashed to smithereens, emitting fizzing sounds like a soda bottle being opened. It seemed to give out some sort of a vapour when it broke into a hundred bits.

At that very instant, a group of warrior monks dressed in white dhotis rushed into the room and surrounded Paati and the children. These were the famous kalari monks of Mounashrampur, trained in the ancient martial art of *kalaripayattu*. They circled Paati and the children, moving gracefully with dance-like movements.

'We are innocent! We are innocent!' Damu yelled desperately. 'We can explain everything. Chanchanachan was trying to poison Mouna Baba with the bright orange cashew nut on the laddoo. That's why Vikram had to hit the laddoo with his catapult! I overheard Dr Nandini and her father Periyaswami discussing it! They were ...' Damu couldn't finish his explanation because the sound of someone giggling filled the room.

It began as a soft giggle. Just a tee-hee-hee. Then it turned into a chuckle. Heh-heh-heh. And just as everyone realised in amazement where the sound was coming from, Chanchanachan burst into a thunderously loud guffaw. Hrah-ha-hah-ha-hah! Chanchanachan was rolling on the ground, clutching his sides and laughing uproariously.

Everyone in the room was staring at Chanchanchan in utter astonishment. What could he possibly be finding so funny?

'It's the Chuckling Gas in the la-doo-hoo-hoo-ha-ha-haaah!' Chanachanachan staggered up weakly, laughing all the while as he explained, 'It's not a poisoned laddoo. It's filled with the herbal Chuckling Gas made by Dr Nandini. She filled a tiny capsule, made from a very thin shell of sugar, with the Chuckling Gas and put it in the laddoo. Chuckling Gas makes people happy when it is inhaled. It makes them laugh uncontrollably! The Chuckling Gas in the laddoo becomes active only when the capsule is broken. I was supposed to break the capsule just before offering the lad-doo-hoo-hooo-haa-haa,' he broke off as he dissolved into another fit of laughter.

'How were you planning to activate the Chuckling Gas in the laddoo? And why did you want to make Mouna Baba laugh?' Damu was curious. 'How strange! So much planning for such a harmless prank!'

'Ha-ha-ha-harmless! You think it's ha-ha-harmless? The effects of this gas last for almost half a day. The gas doesn't just make you laugh.

It relaxes you and makes you talk and sing wildly. What do you think would happen if the Mouna Baba started laughing and talking hysterically today—which is the one day of the year when he meets his devotee-heee-heee-heees. Ha-ha-ha ...'

Everyone in the room had to wait till Chanchanchan stopped laughing and could continue his explanation.

'I was supposed to turn the laddoo upside down with a sharp jerk that would break the capsule and release the Chuckling Gas. It was a clever plan made by Dr Nandini and her father. After inverting the laddoo, I was to leave the tray and walk away quickly so that only the Mouna Baba, and no one else, would be affected by the gas. I was to identify the laddoo by the bright orange cashew nut on it, a cashew dipped in orange food colouring! We tried to carry out the same plan last year. On this same day when Mouna Baba meets his devotees. But that silly wrestler Veerapandi—he ate the laddoo with the Chuckling Gas capsule in it by mistake! It didn't do him any harm though. He-heee-hee-heee-he went on to win the wrestling championship the next day. Eating the gas probably doesn't have the same effect as inhaling it!'

'Something's not sounding right,' Paati said. 'If it's just a prank, why would Nandini go to such lengths to try and steal the formula? Why did she ask Khabardar Khan to try and drown us?'

'Prank! Are you crazy?' The Chuckling Gas was making Chanchanachan talk wildly. 'If the Mouna Baba broke his vow of silence by talking and laughing crazily in front of thousands of his devotees, the ashram would have to ask him step down. He would be disgraced and have to leave the ashram. Then another Mouna Baba would be chosen in his place. Dr Nandini hates this Mouna Baba because he checks the accounts of Mouna Labs personally. That doesn't suit people like her who were stealing from the profits. Nandini is desperate to get rid of our dear Mouna Baba somehow before she is charged with fraud and sent to priss-sss-sss-on. Ha-ha-ha …' The rest of the sentence was lost in wild guffawing.

Mouna Baba gestured to one of the kalari monks to hand him a slate. He wrote something on it and then got up and left the room.

The kalari monk seemed to glide across the floor as he approached Paati and the children. 'Mouna Baba has gone to meet his devotees. He asks you to stay in the ashram till we question

Dr Nandini and her father, Periyaswami.'

He showed Paati the slate on which Mouna Baba had written something in Mounabashalu.

'What does it say Paati?' the children were curious.

'I can't read it too well. I think it says that the kalari monks are supposed to bring Dr Nandini and Periyaswami to the ashram for questioning. They also have to locate Khabardar Khan for questioning. And also … oh no … how could this be?' Paati's face had turned pale.

'What is it Paati? Tell us.'

'It says that if on questioning all these people, it is proved that Chanchanachan and the four of us have been lying, we will have to face charges of trying to attack the Mouna Baba. With a catapult!'

'This is ridiculous! To club us along with that villain Chanchanachan! We try to save Mouna Baba's life and he accuses us of trying to attack him!' Laila was indignant.

'Yes. This is an insult. We are not criminals. We will not stay in this ashram one minute longer. Come, children!' Paati was very annoyed.

'I'm afraid I cannot permit you to leave the ashram till the investigation has been completed,' said the kalari monk, graciously but very firmly. 'Come, I will show you to your rooms.'

The Flying Wrestler

The effects of the Chuckling Gas did wear off by the next morning. And when that happened, Chanchanachan stoutly denied everything that he had said the previous day. He refused to accept that he had ever mentioned any laddoo filled with Chuckling Gas.

Dr Nandini and her father Periyaswami had been called to the ashram. Both of them swore that they knew nothing about the Chuckling Gas in the laddoo.

'Your Holiness,' said Periyaswami, 'all these accusations about some imaginary Chuckling Gas being planted in a laddoo have been made up by Chanchanachan. They are nothing more than lies!'

'And he is not the only one lying. This old lady Mrs Malu and these children are lying too. I have never even heard of herbal Chuckling Gas which can be put in a laddoo This is all a dangerous plot hatched by Chanchanachan and these children to attack your Holiness!' Dr Nandini sounded so sincere that no one in the room could disbelieve her.

All eyes in the room were now turned suspiciously on Paati and the children.

'Respected Mouna Baba, please listen to my entire explanation,' Paati began. 'More than a year ago, I found a secret formula for making wonderful hair oil that can make hair grow even on bald heads. The formula was in a file of my father's papers, sent to me after his death. Some weeks ago, Nandini sent a man called Khabardar Khan to steal the formula from me. But Khabardar could not find the formula because I hid it quite cleverly. So Nandini asked him to prevent us from reaching Mounashrampur with the formula. Even if it meant having to drown us! Why did Nandini want the formula so desperately? Yesterday, I found out. What I had with me was not a formula for making hair oil but the formula for making herbal Chuckling Gas. It was Nandini's formulation and it was in her handwriting. There was also a diagram showing how the gas is activated when the laddoo is turned upside down.'

'Yes, your Holiness,' Damu added, 'I have seen that formula. There are diagrams too. Malu Paati thought it was a picture of a bald man but it was actually a laddoo. We mistook the cashew nut for a sketch of the man's sad mouth. And the second picture was of the laddoo inverted and the gas coming out of it. That's the picture we mistook for the bald man smiling happily as he sprouted hair.'

Paati and the children nodded vigorously in agreement. Damu's explanation made perfect sense to them. But Mouna Baba and the monks looked puzzled. This sounded like utter gibberish.

Mouna Baba wrote something on a slate and one of the Kalari monks read it out, 'I need to see proof of what you are saying. Where is this formula?'

'Er ... er ... the formula is no longer with us, your Holiness. Dr Nandini and Periyaswami took it from us by force. They threatened us with guns. I have no proof to show you but I speak the truth.' Paati was confident she would be believed. No one had ever distrusted her.

'Mouna Baba says that unless he has proof, he can only conclude that you, the children and Chanchanachan were trying to attack him,' the kalari monk read out from the slate after Mouna Baba had written on it.

'I have proof, your Holiness. You don't need to see the formula. I can recite it by heart,' Damu sounded pleased. Paati and the children, who had been getting very worried, cheered up when they heard this. Once Mouna Baba heard the formula, he would have to believe them.

There was some delay because Mouna Baba sent for his own ayurvedic physician who had a vast knowledge of the properties of herbs. He would be able to judge whether the ingredients Damu mentioned could be used for making a gas which made people laugh uncontrollably. When the ayurvedic doctor came, Damu began reciting the formula enthusiastically. 'A drizzle of sea mist, a trickle of honey twists. Six measures of tiger's sighs, 24 scoops of corn eyes.'

When Damu reached 'A litre of marigold milk, 3 skeins of snapdragon silk,' the ayurvedic doctor held up his hand.

'Your Holiness, many of the ingredients mentioned are not known to me. But some of the others are known to have hair growth stimulating properties. This seems to be a formula for making hair oil.'

Every monk in the room was now glaring angrily at Paati and the children.

'It seems quite clear that Mrs Malu and the children along with Chanchanachan are lying!' commented the chief of the kalari monks. 'We will have to charge them with an attempt to attack your Holiness.'

'No, no, please, listen. I did change the

formula a little. The original formula for making the Chuckling Gas was in Mounabashalu, which is a language I can no longer read well. I have omitted some of the ingredients and added some of my own. I could not have possibly used raisins soaked in camel dung!'

'Ahhh! Now camel dung is known to have certain er … er … explosive properties,' the ayurvedic doctor nodded solemnly, 'It does behave like a … whaa …? Did I just see a man in pink and purple polka-dotted shorts parachute into the courtyard?'

The kalari monks ran to the window and reported, 'It is a huge man with a long ponytail carrying a grey backpack. He's demanding to come in!'

'Appa!' exclaimed Damu in relief.

'Veerapandi mama!' piped up two more happy voices.

'Appa must have brought the last piece of the formula. That will be our proof! This piece of the formula contains the key bits of the chemical composition and the diagrams we were talking about!'

Mouna Baba signalled that Veerapandi was to be let in.

It took all of two and a half minutes for

Veerapandi to burst into the room. The delay was because the monks had insisted on lending him a robe to wear over his pink and purple polka-dotted shorts before meeting Mouna Baba.

Veerapandi rushed in and hugged Damu, kissing him on both cheeks several times. He hugged Viks and Laila and then, overcome with emotion, enveloped Paati in a crushing hug too. 'I travelled by air and came as soon as I could. The price of air-tickets has gone up since last year! What an experience it was! This time even my gold tooth-filling fell out on the way.'

'Show Mouna Baba the formula from Viks's backpack,' Paati reminded him gently. The last piece of the formula from Viks's backpack was

handed to Mouna Baba.

Mouna Baba looked carefully at the piece of paper and seemed convinced. He looked sorrowfully at Dr Nandini and Periyaswami, saddened that people in his own lab had plotted to disgrace him. He summoned the chief of the kalari monks to his side.

'This is a frame up. It's just a pack of lies!' Dr Nandini shouted, realising she had been exposed.

Suddenly, there was more noise and excitement in the courtyard.

'Not another person arriving by air, I hope,' said Veerapandi anxiously.

The chief of the kalari monks looked out of the window and reported. 'It's one of my monks. He seems to be bringing two dancing bears with him—you know those poor animals that are dressed up and made to dance. No, wait a minute. Those are not bears! Those are two men. I thought they were bears because they have hair growing all over their faces!'

'Is one of them wearing a yellow T-shirt and bright green trousers?' Viks asked.

'Why yes! Do you know those men?'

'Very well indeed,' said Viks. 'I told you your concentrated Wondergro Supersonic Hair Tonic made hair grow at superfast speed, Paati. That's

Khabardar Khan and the man in the motor boat. Remember how they went back to sleep in the middle of the Singing Grasses with the hair oil smeared all over their faces? So now they have a supersonic growth of hair on their faces!'

The two men were led in. The children burst out laughing, Paati smiled, the lips of the monks twitched in amusement and even the Mouna Baba's eyes twinkled. It was Khabardar Khan and his friend. They had hair growing on every inch of their faces—except their eyeballs!!

When Khabardar spotted Paati and the children, he fell to his knees quaking in fear.

'Aiyyo! Aiyyo! These ghosts are here again to haunt me again! How did they rise from the bottom of the river! I should never have listened to that old witch, Dr Nandini,' he sobbed.

'I think we have all the proof we need,' said the chief of the kalari monks. At a signal from Mouna Baba, all five villains were led away.

Dr Nandini went out yelling how she would get those 'hideously humongous hieroglyphics', Periyaswami and Chanchanachan went quietly, while Khabardar and his partner in crime were dragged out moaning about the 'ghosts' who were haunting them.

The kalari monk was asked to read out Mouna Baba's message to Paati and the children before they left. 'Mouna Baba wishes to thank you all for saving him from disgrace. He apologises deeply for having suspected you. His prayers and good wishes are always with the five of you. As a token of his gratitude, he presents you with a basket of fruits, a box of laddoos, and five air-tickets back to your home town.'

On hearing this, Veerapandi fell to his knees and thumped his chest saying, 'Thank you, Mouna Baba, but I would rather walk back through the Vankozhimozhi Forest. No more air travel for me! Please!'

'Er … the tickets are for travelling by Mouna Baba's private helicopter which is used to transport the very sick patients in Mounashrampur to hospitals in the city,' the kalari monk clarified, with a twinkle in his eye. 'It's a perfectly comfortable way to travel.'

In the helicopter, Veerapandi clutched the box of laddoos tightly. He hadn't eaten since early that morning, when he had started out from home to make the air-trip to Mounashrampur. As soon as the helicopter had taken off, he lifted the lid off the box and offered it to everybody.

Viks took all the laddoos he could hold at one time—seven! Damu picked up two, Paati took one, Laila broke off half for herself leaving just one and a half laddoos in the box for Veerapandi.

Veerapandi took the last laddoo and if it weren't for the seat belt strapping him into his seat, he would surely have fallen out of the helicopter in surprise. For lying in the box, under the last laddoo, was a flat blueish-greenish-silvery-grey stone.

He held it up for everyone in the helicopter to see. 'It's … this is … you know …' Veerapandi was too excited to speak.

'Yes, Appa, we know. It's a lump of magic lava. A gift from Mouna Baba. I wonder how he knew you had lost the one that had been in our family for generations.'

Veerapandi's eyes were too blurred with tears of happiness to notice that Viks had just eaten the last half of the laddoo in the box and was now tucking into the fruit.